The Restaurant Bear

By Colin Taylor

First published in 2011 by New Generation Publishing

First Edition

Book and cover design: Graham Taylor
Artistic advisor: Susanne Taylor

Chapter 1

"Mum! Have you seen my sweets?" Ian's shout echoed from his room down the corridor of the flat they lived in, above *The Bear* restaurant. He walked down to the kitchen to talk to her.

"Have you seen them?"

"No, where did you leave them?" she replied, without looking up from the letters she was reading.

"They were on the shelf in my room. I left them there on Friday, before I went to Vincent's birthday party. Now they're all gone."

"Are you sure you didn't leave them somewhere else?" she asked.

Had he left them anywhere else? No, he was sure he'd left them in his room.

"No," he said. "The box is still on the shelf, but they're all gone."

"Have you asked Rachel if she's seen them?" said Mum.

Perhaps his little sister had sneaked into his room while he was away for the weekend at Vincent's birthday party. Vincent was a friend from where they used to live, before Ian's dad had bought the restaurant.

Ian went to Rachel's room and shoved the door open. He looked around the pink room, hoping to see the sweets or at least the wrappers, somewhere amongst Rachel's toys stacked neatly on her shelves, although he didn't really think she'd be silly enough to leave evidence like that around.

He wondered again why Rachel always had to have everything pink. Did she do it just to annoy him?

"Did you eat my sweets?" he demanded.

Rachel looked up from her dolls on the carpet at Ian's angry face. She scowled and shook her head violently, her wavy dark brown hair swirling around her shoulders.

"No! Go away." He wandered out.

"Mum…?" His mum was walking along the hallway.

"No luck then?" He shook his head.

"Perhaps it's the same person who took the sausages and burgers from the fridge," said his mum.

"Yeah, but you've put a lock on it now."

Since they had moved to *The Bear* restaurant in Branchester, Ian had sometimes sneaked down to the restaurant kitchen and taken leftover food from the fridge for a midnight feast. Never uncooked meat though, and nothing anyone would notice.

Ian wondered who had taken the sausages and burgers. If he knew, he'd make them give all the food back, or maybe tell the police. For a minute he dreamed of being a hero, except that as his mum said, the police had got better things to do than listen to ten-year-old boys.

His long legs carried him quickly along the corridor and downstairs to the restaurant kitchen. Dad didn't like to be disturbed when he was preparing food with the other chefs, but this was important, someone was stealing his sweets!

His father was not impressed and sent him away.

"Not now! Later. I'm busy. Can't you see?"

The words echoed in Ian's ears. Why did grownups always say that? You know they're not going to remember, or have any time later.

Ian wandered through the restaurant. He wasn't supposed to do that either, even though the restaurant was closed in the morning. As he walked down the main aisle between the tables, he looked up, straight at the stuffed bear's head hanging on the wall, which gave *The Bear* restaurant its name.

It was strange how it always seemed to look straight back at him. Of course it wasn't really looking at him – it was dead. He knew that, but sometimes he would hide amongst the tables and pretend to hunt it with an imaginary rifle.

Other times he thought of it as an alien and had fights with it. He always won, and would give orders for it to be turned into a trophy and hung on the wall. He laughed when he thought of what his sister would say. She loved animals.

Ian sometimes wondered where it had come from and how old it was. It looked pretty ancient to him. He liked it though. It had a friendly look about it.

Was it a he or a she? It was hard to know. Could you tell from its face? He'd look it up on the internet sometime, if his parents ever got round to having it installed. He wandered out through the back door into the garden.

Everyone else was in bed when Ian crept down the stairs in the dark. He counted in a whisper as he went:

"... seven, eight, nine, miss ten, eleven, twelve, thirteen, fourteen, fifteen, miss sixteen." He stopped. Where had that creak come from?

Had he counted wrongly? No he always got it right. Whenever he came down to raid the fridge at night, he knew which steps to miss so they wouldn't creak.

Counting was easy. He'd been counting ever since the infants. He was in the top group for maths at school, his old school that is. Ian wondered what the new one would be like.

A strange school and new children made him feel nervous. It wasn't as if he'd made any new friends yet. Living above the restaurant in the high street meant there weren't any other children living nearby.

Would the children in his new year six class like him? The thought slipped from his mind as he heard the noise again. This time it sounded as if it had come from the direction of the restaurant kitchen. What if it was the thief?

He froze. What should he do?

It didn't occur to him to be frightened. If he woke up his mum and dad, by the time he'd explained to them, the thief would be gone, even if they did believe him. He was too little to capture a thief. This wasn't pretending or boasting with his mates. What could he do?

Aha! Silently he rushed back upstairs and, just as quietly, returned with the disposable camera he'd been given for Christmas. He'd wanted a phone camera as a present, but dad had said no, he was too young, maybe next year.

Never mind, if he could take a picture of the thief he'd have proof. They would have to believe him then and his dad would have to do something about it. Maybe his dad would call the police, or if it were one of the restaurant staff, perhaps they'd get the sack.

He nearly laughed then. He knew it was nothing to do with sacks really, it meant they lost their job, but he got a funny picture in his head anyway. The thought of a sack on someone's head almost made him laugh out loud.

He walked quietly down the stairs, counting inside his head this time. He didn't want to disturb the thief before he could get a picture. What would he do when the flash went off? Rush upstairs and tell Mum and Dad straight away.

He wouldn't tell them that he was there to take food from the fridge himself. If they thought he knew where the key was, they'd move it. He'd just heard something and had gone to investigate.

As he got closer to the bottom of the stairs he could hear very faint noises coming from the kitchen: strange scuffling sounds. He moved slowly down the dark, wood-panelled corridor, towards the half open kitchen door at the end. Just a few more steps and he was there. He peeped around the door carefully, not knowing what to expect.

It was very dark. He could just see a big black shape by the fridge. The shape pulled at the fridge door and made little grunting noises with the effort. Ian couldn't see who it was.

He needed the shape to turn round so he could get a picture of its face. Picking a big serving spoon off the nearby rack with one hand and taking careful aim with the camera in the other hand, he dropped the metal spoon.

Time slowed. The spoon took an age to fall to the tiled floor. Suddenly for the first time he felt afraid. What if the person managed to catch him before he could escape? He made a grab at the spoon.

Too late! His hand was also moving in slow motion. Clang! The spoon hit the floor as he pressed the camera button, not knowing if he had taken a good picture or not. What if he'd tilted the camera?

With the flash came a terrible, deep-throated cry like the cats fighting by the dustbins. Without looking back Ian raced out of the kitchen.

As he rushed up the stairs, he heard his parents' bedroom door fly open. There was the click of the light switch and here was his father, in blue striped pyjamas, without his glasses, brown hair tousled from sleep, coming out of the bedroom shouting questions.

"What's all this noise about? What are you doing out of bed? Why were you downstairs?"

Ian stood a moment, thinking quickly.

"I woke up. I heard a noise from downstairs. I thought it might be the food thief in the kitchen. I went to look and it was. He chased me. He was big and dressed in black clothes." The thought of being chased made him feel frightened now. What if the thief had managed to grab him!

Tears blinked into his green eyes and his face paled under its summer tan. His father stared at him in astonishment. His mother appeared behind his father, pulling on her flowery dressing gown.

"Are you sure it wasn't a dream?" she asked. "You know what you're like with your nightmares."

"Mum, it wasn't. Honest."

"Phil, go and have a look."

"All right dear. Stay here," he ordered, looking at Ian.

Mum yawned and put an arm around Ian's shoulders. They could hear Dad moving around downstairs. He came back up.

"There's nothing there. Just a big serving spoon lying on the floor. It must've fallen off the rack somehow. That's what you heard, Ian." Then he spoke quietly to his wife. "It's just his imagination. Sleepwalking maybe."

"Perhaps it was just a dream, Ian," suggested Mum.

"But it wasn't, Mum, really."

"Look," said Dad, "there's nothing there, Ian. I've checked. All the doors are locked, no windows broken. We're all quite safe, so let's all go back to bed. Now, before you wake your sister up."

Ian knew it was no good arguing, they wouldn't believe him, but he'd show them.

He had proof.

Neither of his parents had noticed the camera he held by his side. He was about to say something, when he thought, what if he'd pointed the camera in the wrong direction when he'd tried to grab the spoon. He might not have taken a picture of the thief. He'd better wait until the film was developed. He was almost sure he'd got a good photo and if he had then his parents would have to listen to him.

Ian turned to go to his room.

"Oh, and go and take all those magnetic letters off the fridge in the morning and give them back to Rachel. I asked her to do it, but she keeps forgetting," said Dad.

"What! Why can't she do it?"

"Look Ian, just do it, before you forget. I've had enough of your strange messages to each other. If you want help with something why can't you just ask each other? There's no need to leave messages all over the fridge."

Messages? He hadn't left messages anywhere. Seeing his dad's irritable look he thought he'd better not say so.

"Yes, dad," he said and sighed.

Next morning he got up early, walked slowly down the stairs and peeped round the kitchen door to make sure there was nobody there.

He looked at the magnetic letters on the enormous fridge door. They'd been there when they bought the restaurant. It had been Rachel's favourite thing to make words with them when they first arrived. He didn't know she was still doing it.

HLEP ME IAN
BEER

Hlep me Ian. What was that supposed to mean? Oh she meant help me. Huh! I'm not helping her with anything.

13

And what's beer got to do with it anyway?

HELP THE BIR RACHL

Bir? What was that? Why was Rachel doing such strange things? Little sisters. Ian would never understand them. Picking up a plastic bag he put all the letters in it and went back up to his room.

Chapter 2

"These are yours. Dad told me to give them to you."

Ian plonked the bag of magnetic letters down on the kitchen table in front of Rachel. He was supposed to have given them to her last week. He wasn't telling her that. She looked in the bag as if there might be something alive inside.

"They're not mine. I don't want them."

"Well, you're the one who keeps writing messages with them. And you can't spell."

"I can spell. I'm brilliant. And I haven't touched those letters for weeks. Leave me alone."

"Dad told me to give them to you. So I've done it. I don't care what you do with them."

Mum entered the kitchen. "I do wish you two would stop squabbling. You used to be such good friends. Here, Ian. These are yours."

Mum passed him the wallet of photographs.

"Thanks Mum," he said, eagerly taking it from her. "Have you looked at them?"

She shook her head, laughing. "I wouldn't dare, would I? You must have told me at least fifty times that you had to be the first to see them."

"Aren't you going to look at them then?" Rachel asked him curiously.

"Yes, I am, but nowhere near you. I'm going."

In his room he carefully undid the flap and opened the wallet. For a moment he stopped, wondering, almost afraid. What if he hadn't taken a photo of the thief? What if he had and it was someone he knew, or even liked?

He shook his head like a dog shaking off water. He had to know one way or the other. Slipping his hand into the wallet, he pulled the photos out. The top ones were from last Christmas, when he'd been given the camera.

There was Aunt Mary and Uncle Grant in one, both laughing at him, but Uncle Grant only had half a head! There were two with big blobby things across the pictures and little stickers saying how important it was to keep fingers away from the lens when taking photographs.

There were some brilliant ones of him and Rachel opening the rest of their presents. Mum had taken those. The pictures at Vincent's party were good too, especially the ones at the pool when they threw Vincent in. There were several of the house and others of his room and some he'd taken out of the window.

He was beginning to think that the thief one might not have come out, when suddenly he froze, staring in surprise at the last photograph.

Was this the thief?

It wasn't possible. How could it be? They must have sent him the wrong photographs. No, the kitchen was in the background and there, in the middle of the picture, one paw around the fridge, the other holding the door handle, staring right at him, was a bear. A big, dark brown, red-eyed, bear! He placed the photograph on his bed and stared at it.

A bear. This was crazy. It must be someone playing a trick, wearing a bear suit – it couldn't really be a bear. How could a bear… The thought trailed off in his mind. A bear! The restaurant bear!

But that was just a head and it was dead. This was a whole bear. Well almost, he couldn't see the legs. The picture only showed the bear from the waist up.

He looked closely. It was strange. It looked just like the restaurant bear, and yet, somehow, it didn't. The restaurant bear was dead. This bear was alive, like the ones you see in the zoo.

Ian looked at the picture on his bed and thought for a while. He couldn't tell his mum and dad he'd taken a photograph of the thief now. They would never, ever believe him.

Picking up the photograph he slipped it into his back pocket. He shuffled the rest back into their folder, threw them onto his bedside cabinet, walked to the door and quietly opened it. He started to go downstairs and stopped. He could hear people in the restaurant. They were having lunch. It would be hours before they finished and he wasn't allowed in the restaurant when there were customers. Dad had said. But he had to have a look at the bear.

Maybe he could creep in somehow. He walked towards the back door, past the noisy kitchen. The smell of the different dishes coming through the cracks in the doors and windows made him feel hungry.

He wished he could have a proper dinner when he was home during the holidays, like he did at school in term time, and not just a snack. He knew Mum had no time during the day; she had to manage the customer area, while Dad was just as busy as he cooked and supervised the other chefs in the kitchen.

If Dad had kept his old chef's job, instead of using the money he got when Gran died to buy the restaurant, maybe Ian would get more attention. He sighed. They just didn't have much time for him anymore. They were always so tired and they worked so hard. He knew that. They said things would get better and it would be good for them all when the restaurant made lots of money.

But they weren't going to have a holiday this summer because of the restaurant. Instead Mum had said he could go and stay at Auntie Jean's, down at Bognor Regis, for a week. She hadn't got around to arranging it yet though, and there were only two weeks of the summer holidays left now.

He put thoughts of going on holiday out of his mind. He had to find out about the bear.

Going out of the back door, he turned right into the yard, went up the alley, unbolted the side gate and peeped round. He looked at the restaurant, with its green and red painted front and big hanging sign with the bear's head painted on it.

No one was there. Crouching down below the big windows he quickly shuffled along to the entrance doors. Carefully, so as not to be seen, he looked through the glass panel. The restaurant was full, but no one was waiting. He pushed the swing door open slightly, slipped in and ducked down beside the old fashioned reception desk. There was just room for him to squeeze underneath and not be seen.

He studied the bear's head hung on the wall at the other end of the restaurant, above the dark wooden panelling that ran all around the walls. Pulling the photograph of the bear out of his pocket, he looked at it. He glanced back at the wall and then he took another look at the head in the photograph, and then back at the wall again.

The eyes looked the same!

The ears looked the same!

What else was there? Teeth! Yes, how many teeth did it have? He counted them in the photo, starting from the left of its mouth. Got it! One tooth was shorter than the rest. Perhaps it was broken off. Now he'd know for sure. He knew it wouldn't be the same. Things like that just didn't happen in real life. It was fun trying to find out though. He looked at the bear's head once more. It was too far away. He couldn't see the teeth properly. If only he'd brought his telescope with him.

Because the restaurant was crowded it was very noisy. All the waiters and waitresses, in their black and white uniforms, were busy and he couldn't see Mum anywhere. Would they notice if he crawled around by the front window and hid behind the curtains?

If any of the staff saw him, he knew they'd say to Dad,

and Dad had promised he'd do more than just tell Ian off this time. He got really angry before, went all red in the face and shouted at him.

Ian didn't really see why it mattered. It was not as if he did any damage or upset the customers or anything. Grownups didn't always need reasons though, he'd learnt that. They just did things and bossed you about. It had been much more fun before they bought the restaurant.

A big sigh slipped from his lips. Perhaps he should go and not take a chance. He could come back tonight when it was dark and there was no one about.

No! How could he possibly wait until tonight? He had to know, even if he was caught. It couldn't be the same bear. That would be silly, but what if it was? A shiver of excitement shot up his spine. He had to know now!

Moving slowly out of the cramped space under the table, so as not to attract attention, he started to crawl around the edge of the long curved front window. The sounds of the restaurant – cutlery, plates and customers eating, drinking and talking – was louder here, but he seemed to be moving in his own time bubble, everything else was dim and far away.

He headed for the curtains at the other end of the room. No one seemed to be paying any attention to him. They were far too busy eating Dad's wonderfully tasty meals and all the waiters and waitresses were taking orders, delivering food or presenting bills.

At last he reached the curtains. He disappeared quietly behind their red and green patterns, breathing slowly until his heart stopped beating so fast. He peeped around the edge of the long material.

He could see the bear easily from here. Now he had to check the teeth. Of course he knew they would be different to the photo picture. He didn't believe in fairy stories or magic, he was much too sensible for that!

He glanced at the photograph, just to make sure he knew what he was looking for, and stared at the bear's head. Now he had another problem. Because he was almost sideways on to the bear, it was more difficult to count the teeth on the other side. Perhaps he could see more easily if he stood up.

That was better.

He leaned forward to get a better view, putting a hand out to steady himself as he counted. His arm brushed against a pot plant. It slid along the polished wooden windowsill and fell down onto the carpet. That only made a little noise. The metal saucer it had been standing on rolled along the carpet, out onto the shiny wooden floor like a tiny wheel, stopping against a customer's table with a loud CLANG!

Oh no! He'd be caught! Quickly he scuttled around the edge of the room again. If only he could get under the desk fast enough, maybe they wouldn't see him.

The whole room had stopped and looked to see what the noise was. Luckily, the metal saucer had rolled in the opposite direction from him. They were all looking the other way.

He was safe. They hadn't seen him. He ducked under the desk, out the other side and back by the main door. Then down the alley, through the yard and out into the garden, not stopping until he reached his favourite tree and was sitting amongst its branches.

His heart was pounding. He looked in the direction of the restaurant. No one coming, no one shouting, he was safe and what's more, now he knew. He had counted the teeth just before he'd knocked the plant over.

And he couldn't believe it, they were exactly the same. With one broken tooth in just the same place. The bear in the photograph was *definitely* the restaurant bear.

Chapter 3

Ian looked at the bear's head in the torchlight. With the restaurant closed for the night, and everyone in bed, he had come down to see for sure. There was the broken tooth, exactly the same as the photograph.

What did it mean? How could a dead bear come alive? Magic? No such thing. How could there be? That was just pretend, special effects, like on TV and films. Perhaps he was dreaming it.

He pointed at the bear accusingly.

"Was it you took my sweets? 'Cos if it was how did you get down and turn into a real bear? Oh, this is stupid. I'm talking to a dead bear."

He yawned.

"I'm going to bed and if anything else goes missing I'll tell my mum and dad and they'll put you in the bin. So there."

The bear had always looked so friendly in the daytime. It looked different at night. Not scary though. It just seemed a bit sad.

He walked away slowly towards the door and turned to take another look.

He blinked. It was smiling! He stared. Was it? It couldn't be. He was imagining things. Just like his mum said.

The stone floor was cold on his bare feet. He pulled

his dressing gown around him and opened the door. He turned and was about to say goodnight to the bear. Instead his mouth dropped open, icy shivers rushing up his spine, making his short brown hair feel like it was standing on end.

There on the wall, in the beam of the torch, was the large wooden shield shape the bear hung on, but the bear's head had gone. Oh no!

He shone the torch around. A big black shape was bounding towards him, between the tables. Ian stood rooted to the spot.

It was then that he fainted. He knew what fainting was. It was when people fell over, like they'd fallen asleep on their feet, except it wasn't being asleep. It was something to do with the blood not getting to your brain. He knew that it didn't hurt, unless you bumped yourself when you fell over and that you woke up afterwards and just felt dizzy. Then you'd be all right. He knew that.

What he didn't expect was to wake up with a bear cuddling him in its arms, asking him if he was feeling better in a strange, deep, growly voice. She hadn't wanted to frighten him and she wasn't always sure when to turn into a real bear because people ran away if she did and they thought she was a ghost or something and sometimes the magic worked a bit quickly and when he had started to leave she had been so anxious to talk to him before he went, she'd simply rushed over in the end. Her name was Rosa. Would he like a drink of water?

"No thank you," said Ian. "Are you a lady bear then?"

"I'm not a bear at all!" said the smiling bear.

"Yes you are," said Ian. He touched the bear. The fur felt smooth and soft. It was nice. He was over his fright now.

"You feel all nice," he said. "How did you get off the wall? Is it magic?"

He wanted to say, "Are you real?" That was a little difficult though, it sounded a bit rude. So instead he said accusingly.

"You ate my sweets, and the sausages from the fridge. You did, didn't you? I took a photo of you."

"Yes," agreed the bear. "I am sorry. The magic makes me no need to eat, but sometimes, when I wander around the restaurant, the bear part of me wants meat and sweet things. The sweets tasted so wonderful. I thank you for them."

"That's all right," Ian smiled. "Mum gave me money for more in the end. I did some jobs for her in the flat. You'd better not do it again though, or they might get suspicious."

Then he thought of something else.

"And it was you who wrote the messages with the magnet letters. You didn't spell it right. I didn't understand."

"I tried all things for you helping me. My English is not so good."

"It's good enough."

He smiled. I'm talking to a bear about her spelling, he thought.

"I'm not dreaming you, am I?" he said.

The bear laughed. A deep grumbly, growly sound that

25

made her whole body shake.

"No," she said. "I'm quite real. It's a long, complicated story. You would call me a witch. But I'm really a wise woman."

"A witch?" exclaimed Ian. "There's no such thing as witches."

Now he really must be dreaming.

Still holding him, the bear explained. It took a long while and the bear was so warm and cuddly that Ian, without the bear realising it, fell fast asleep.

After a while the bear looked down at him in the pale moonlight shining through the high front windows of the restaurant. The torch had long ago gone out. Ian had dropped it when he fainted and the bear had picked it up. She smiled a bear-like smile.

Silently the bear gathered him up in her arms, stood up and, with only a few clicks of her claws, took him up the stairs into his room. She laid him on his bed, pulled the covers over him, smoothed down his hair with one big paw, gently gave him a lick on his cheek for a kiss, and crept down to the restaurant again.

She looked around and with a sound like a tap being turned on hard, she flowed up onto the wall. In a moment she was just a head again, silently looking down at the lonely rows of empty tables in the restaurant by the light of the silvery moon still shining through the restaurant windows.

Chapter 4

It was Sunday. They always had breakfast early on a Sunday. Ian and Rachel had to get up and they sat round the kitchen table.

"Like a proper family," said Mum.

Ian and Rachel knew there would be no Sunday television if they didn't eat together and Mum made delicious breakfasts anyway, so it wasn't too hard to get up.

It was while he was eating his second boiled egg that Rachel did it. She said very loudly and clearly, "Ian talks to the bear on the wall."

His hand jerked. The egg that had been about to go into his open mouth fell off his spoon. It slid down his chin, dropping onto his front, leaving a yellow yolk trail on his blue dressing gown.

Dad looked up from the newspaper and said, "Pardon?" Mum looked at Ian and passed him a napkin. Ian went bright red as he wiped at the egg.

"He does. I've seen him lots of times."

Rachel sat there, her hazel eyes glaring at Ian, her pale face determined. There was no hint of laughter about her red lips beneath her sharp little nose. Mum looked in surprise at her set expression and laughed softly. She glanced at Dad and then replied.

"That's all right, Ian. You always did have an active imagination. When I was young I talked to my dolls. No one minded. And Rachel, it's not very nice to talk about private things to everyone. Ian's not doing anything wrong, and besides, you talk to your toys too, sometimes."

Rachel was about to say, "But he says it comes alive," when Ian managed to knock over the orange juice, most of it going towards Mum. Everyone had to move while Mum took the cloth off the table and put it into the washing machine.

Ian took his chance and followed Rachel as she went out of the room. She knew he was following and started running towards her room, but Ian was quicker.

He got to her door before she could slam it on him. He was really angry now. He didn't shout. He knew Mum and Dad would be listening out for that. He went to grab her arm. She twisted away and ran round to the other side of the bed.

"Don't you dare hurt me or I'll scream and Dad will come and you'll be in trouble again."

Ian stopped. She was right. She always got him into trouble. Why were little sisters always so horrible?

"Leave me alone then. What did you want to go and tell on me for? I didn't do anything to you."

This wasn't true. Rachel had only been horrible to him since he put her best doll on the bonfire at the No-

29

vember 5th firework party last year. He'd only wanted to see how it would melt. A science experiment, really. Until then they'd got along quite well together.

"You burnt my dolly," she had accused.

He'd said sorry ages ago and he wished he hadn't done it. She was always trying to get her revenge on him.

"If you don't say what you're doing with the bear I'm going to tell on you and tell them you say it comes alive, and they'll think you've gone mad and they'll throw it away or burn it or something."

Ian went pale. "You mustn't! You can't! Rosa will never get turned back otherwise and she'll be dead forever and won't get back to Spain." He sounded desperate.

She looked at him as if he really was mad. He'd done it now. He'd have to tell her everything and show her Rosa. So he told her, not everything that Rosa had told him, that had taken every night for a week, just the main part.

He didn't think she would believe him, it was such a strange, complicated story, but Rachel listened, sitting on the bed, open-mouthed with amazement.

The story started quite a while ago, Rosa wasn't sure when. Maybe even over a hundred years ago. She was Romany, a gypsy traveller and had lived in Spain. She was learning to be a Wise Woman, what we would call a witch, but a good witch not a bad witch.

Sometimes at night she had to leave her horse drawn caravan and go up into the mountains and be with her spirit guide, her teacher, so she could teach her things.

She had to change into a bear to talk to her spirit guide, because her spirit guide was the Great Bear in the sky.

Ian hadn't really understood this bit. Rosa kept on talking about Ursa, which was her spirit guide's name, and how you could see her shining up in the sky on a clear night.

It was while she was a big, beautiful bear that something dreadful had happened.

She had been with Ursa all night and was walking down through the trees in the early morning, enjoying being a bear. The golden sun had just come up, casting giant tree shadows across the path.

Suddenly there was a loud bang and she felt a terrific thump on her chest. She fell over and everything went black. The next thing she remembered was being in a castle on the wall. It took a while for her to work out what had happened.

It was the hunting season. There had been lots of hunters in the mountain forests. They couldn't shoot her at night. Daylight was different though. She hadn't meant to be with Ursa for so long that night. The sun had come up and they had shot her and killed her. Then they had cut her head off and stuck it on a big wooden shield to hang on the wall as a trophy.

It was terrible. What could she do?

Her magic stopped her being dead, but she could only come truly alive at night. She had no idea where she had been taken and her magic wasn't strong enough to change her back into a person again.

She needed to speak to the Great Bear Spirit. Ursa

would be able to help her, but something was wrong, Ursa didn't reply. Rosa hadn't known what to do. It had been very lonely sometimes, with no one for her to talk to. When she had tried talking to people at night, as a bear, they would run away, frightened, thinking she was some sort of ghost or had escaped from the zoo or something. Then the people who owned the castle moved.

They had come all the way to England to live, taking Rosa's head with them. Learning to speak English by listening to English people talk was hard. She was beginning to understand when she was taken down and sold, ending up in the restaurant.

Ever since then she had waited, learning more and more English, hoping that someone would come along who could help her change back into a human.

If Rachel was very good, Ian would come and get her that night and would introduce her to Rosa. This was a fabulous adventure. This was a magnificent quest. And they were the ones who would do it. Together they would save Rosa.

But it wasn't going to be as easy as Ian thought.

Chapter 5

There was no moon. It had rained all day and now the clouds spread the darkness of night into every corner. The torch beam shone like a powerful search-light as they went slowly down the stairs, Ian making sure that Rachel didn't step on the creaky ones.

They walked along the corridor and through the swing doors into the restaurant, Rachel holding Ian's hand. All thoughts of getting revenge on him for her doll were forgotten. The restaurant at night was a strange, slightly scary place.

Ian yawned. All these nights without proper sleep, while he visited Rosa, had left him feeling very tired. It was exciting though.

He shone the torch and saw that Rosa was still on the wall, above the pretend fireplace. As he looked, the bear's head seemed to shimmer, like sun on a gently sparkling sea. Slowly, she flowed down onto the floor like a big, brown, furry waterfall.

Rachel stared, holding Ian's hand tightly, clutching at his arm with her free hand and moving behind him for safety. A little *oh* sound escaped from her lips.

Rosa walked towards them on her hind legs and spoke in that strange, deep, bear's voice that Ian was already used to. It had been difficult to understand at first, especially because Rosa was from Spain. She kept saying Spanish words and Ian didn't always know what she meant.

"Ian, this is your little sister? What is your name, little one?" Rachel said nothing and did not move.

"Rachel," said Ian.

"What a beautiful nina she is. Come and give me a hug, nina."

"What's a nin ya?" asked Rachel, saying the unfamiliar word slowly, as if to understand it more easily.

"Why, you are my little nina, my little girl," explained Rosa. Rachel still held tightly onto Ian's hand, squeezing hard. "The nina is frightened?"

A low, bubbling noise came from her throat as Rosa laughed. Moving slowly, she touched Rachel's hand with her furry arm.

"Oh! You're soft," said Rachel. She smiled. "You feel so nice."

Rachel left Ian's side and reached out to Rosa, as she did when she wanted a cuddle. She pressed against Rosa's soft, bulgy body. Sinking into the smooth, glistening fur, she almost seemed to disappear. Rosa let out a big, rumbling sigh and hugged Rachel.

"I think we will like each other, nina." Rachel laughed

as Rosa tickled her.

Ian stood watching, jealousy written on his face. His usually open expression was clouded: a frown line on his forehead. His thin mouth was set in a straight line of disapproval. Rosa was his bear. She had needed his help. Now Rachel had spoilt it.

For a moment he wished he hadn't told her. Until Rosa noticed his expression and reached out, pulling him in too, giving them both such an affectionate bear hug that their breath was quite squeezed away.

"There is love enough for both of you," she said to Ian, stroking his hair with a huge paw. "I am so happy you are here to help me. I have been lonely for so long. All those people around me and no one to talk to."

She sat down on her huge bottom and held them, one on each knee. "Ian, you have found me what I need?"

"I can get the rosemary. Mum keeps those cooking herbs in the kitchen. They're dried though. Does that make any difference?"

"That will do," rumbled the bear. "What about the osopata, my Spanish herb?"

"I don't know what it is yet. I tried looking it up in a herb book, but it only had English ones. Doesn't it have a proper name?"

"What are you talking about?" whispered Rachel sharply to Ian.

"I've got to get things for Rosa. I told you, didn't I? She's not really a bear; she wants to change back into a person. She needs them for the spell."

"Oh," said Rachel. Being held by a real bear, a magic

bear, was lovely but it took some getting used to. She was only just getting used to being downstairs at night.

Rosa was so soft, cuddly and beautiful; Rachel knew it wasn't a dream. Rosa looked real, she felt real and what's more, she smelt real! Just like a wild animal at the zoo, a dog-like smell, only nicer: strong and somehow sweet.

When she had made Ian tell her about Rosa it had just seemed like a wonderful game. A fantastic story, not something that was real. It *was* real though and she *was* getting used to it. She snuggled down a bit more and whispered to Ian.

"Doesn't she like being a bear, then?" Rachel had often imagined herself as an animal. She liked the thought of being a bear.

Rosa laughed. She had a bear's keen sense of hearing too. The rumbly noise made her whole body vibrate. Rachel wriggled.

"Don't! It tickles," she giggled.

"I am not a bear," said Rosa. "Ian, did you not tell her of what we must do to turn me back into a mujer, a woman?"

Ian sighed. He hadn't told Rachel that. How could you tell your little sister you were collecting herbs and earth and stones and things to help turn a bear back into a person? Not even a real bear either, but one that was just a head and came alive at night: a bear that spoke English and hugged you. Rachel was six. She was in year two at school. He knew she had only half believed his story anyway. She wouldn't have understood.

"I told her some things."

"You must tell her everything. You will need her helping to do this."

"Tell me what?" whispered Rachel again. She didn't feel she could speak out loud at this time of night.

"Rosa's not really a bear. She's a witch. Sorry, I mean she's a wise woman."

Rosa didn't like being called a witch. She always said she was a wise woman who only did good things. Ian didn't mind that. A witch sounded a bit scary anyway.

He told Rachel that Rosa needed some things, leaving out all the details that Rosa had told him during the week.

"What sort of things do you need to turn back into a lady then?" asked Rachel.

"I said before." Ian interrupted. "Rosemary, the herb dad puts in with the meat sometimes. I've got that. There's earth from the garden and some stones; I got them with the earth. They don't have to be a special sort or anything, and glasses to put the things in. I can get them from the kitchen when we need them; Mum will never notice any are missing. They've got loads. Oh and candles: four candles."

Ian paused.

"What about the crystal, Ian? You see, Rachel; I need a crystal to focus the energy, to make it all work."

"Sorry Rosa, I forgot. I don't know where we're going to get that from either. Then there's this special Spanish herb, osopata. Only Rosa doesn't know what it's called in English. She can't draw it with her paws and I don't know what to look for because the only name Rosa knows is Spanish and she's never seen it written down. I've looked in all the books in the bookcase," Ian sounded a bit fed up.

Rachel looked thoughtful for a moment.

"Why don't you draw it then? You're so good at art." A look of amazement passed over Ian's face. He hadn't thought of that.

"You are a clever nina. Ian, you must be so happy to have a clever sister with such a good idea," said Rosa.

Ian said nothing. Trust Rachel to think of it. She always showed him up. Why hadn't he thought of it? Still, she was right. He looked around. No pencil or paper down here, he'd have to go upstairs to his room.

"Wait here Rachel, I'll go and get my sketch book."

At the door he looked back. Rachel had snuggled down into Rosa's fur and was looking up at her face and talking excitedly.

As he walked his face creased up into his jealous expression. He hadn't wanted to tell Rachel his secret. Rosa was his bear. Now he'd have to share her.

Still, Rachel had said he was good at drawing. He smiled to himself in the dark. Art and football, he was good at both of them and the art was coming in very handy, though he doubted if the football could help.

He wondered if he would get into the school team at his new school next week. That depended on how good the other boys were, of course. This was a bigger school though. It might not be so easy.

Having found the pad and his pencil case, he returned to the restaurant once more. As he got near to the door he could hear a delighted shriek from Rachel and then she laughed, loudly!

He rushed in. "Sh! You'll wake Mum and Dad," he whispered fiercely. Where were they? He shone the torch around.

There they were. Rachel was riding Rosa between the tables like a horse. She was clinging onto Rosa's thick neck fur with one hand and waving the other one around like a bareback horse-rider in the circus.

"Get down Rachel, I've got to do this drawing," he commanded. Rachel looked across at him and sighed crossly. It was just like Ian to spoil her fun, always acting like a big brother.

She slid down, holding onto Rosa's thick fur, and walked over to Ian's stern face and folded arms. Rosa padded over, looking thoughtfully at Ian's angry face, but saying nothing.

It took a long while for Rosa to describe the herb and for Ian to draw it. Rosa seemed to change her mind all the time about how it looked. She didn't have the right words in English and kept using Spanish ones instead.

Ian was getting fed up and frustrated, but as Rosa said, people in restaurants didn't often talk about herbs and what they looked like, unless they were in the food with the meat and vegetables, that is.

Eventually it was done. It had taken six pages and lots of rubbing out. Rachel was asleep on the carpet and Ian was almost asleep on his chair. Rosa was happy though and as Ian said, now they had a picture, they could start looking.

Would Rosa mind if they didn't come to see her for a while? Mum had been asking him if he was having problems going to sleep, because he kept getting up late and yawning all the time.

But exactly a week later, Ian and Rachel still hadn't found the osopata and school started in two days' time. Worse still, they had some terrible news to tell Rosa.

Chapter 6

What would Rosa think? What would she say? How were they going to tell her? Oh, why did this have to happen?

It was last Tuesday morning. The holidays were nearly over. School started again on Thursday and Ian and Rachel were feeling nervous. They hadn't met any children yet. Living above a restaurant and moving in the holidays had meant that neither of them had been able to make any friends so far.

The restaurant was in the middle of town, on the high street. There were plenty of shops, but not many houses with children in. They had a garden behind the restaurant yard to play in and there was a park beyond that.

Mum had said they weren't allowed to go round the front of the restaurant. They were still not old enough to be alone near such a busy road, especially with the car park opposite, with all those cars going in and out. She had said she'd take them to the park sometime, but she hadn't done that yet.

There hadn't been time to organise trips out anywhere to meet other children, because Mum and Dad were working so hard. As for the holiday with Aunt Jean, Mum must have forgotten about it.

Anyway, this Tuesday morning, Mum and Dad seemed very pleased with themselves. They sat together after breakfast. There was no rushing straight off to the kitchens to prepare for the day. That was unusual.

Dad was smiling at them. What was going on? Suddenly Dad spoke. "Shall we tell them then?"

"Tell us what?" asked Rachel.

"Is it something nice?" said Ian.

They both looked nervous and not just because of school starting. The last time Mum and Dad had spoken to them like this, they'd had to leave all their friends and the old house and move to the restaurant.

"Yes. Why not. Don't look worried, it's good news."

Mum smiled at their wondering faces.

"The restaurant has been doing very well. Very well indeed," continued Dad.

"That's your excellent cooking, dear," praised Mum.

"And your clever organisation and publicity, darling."

Rachel and Ian looked at each other. Why were Mum and Dad getting so soppy?

"When we bought the restaurant it wasn't doing too well. We only had just enough money to buy it. Now business is really good we can get a loan from the bank and do what we really wanted to do in the first place."

He paused a moment and looked at them.

"We're redecorating the whole restaurant, new wallpaper, new paint, new carpets and new furniture. We're getting rid of all that dark panelling on the walls.

Everything will be new and wonderful. And we're giving it a new name too: *The Grand*. The decorators start in six weeks' time. Isn't that fantastic?" He stopped, grinning excitedly at them.

Ian stared.

"What! Everything! Change everything? But what about Rosa?"

"Rosa?" Dad said, puzzled.

"The restaurant bear!"

"Is that what you call it? I know you play with it, but I didn't know it had a name," Dad laughed. "I expect that'll be the first thing in the skip. Good riddance, mangy old thing." Ian stared in disbelief.

"You can't, Dad. You mustn't throw her away," pleaded Rachel, her voice shaking and her eyes almost tearful.

"Why ever not?" asked Mum. "It's only a tatty old head. It stares down at you as if it was still alive." She shivered. "It's horrible. I'm sure it scares the customers. I didn't know you liked it."

Ian tried to say something. The words seemed to stick in his throat. How could he tell grownups about their magic bear that only came alive at night? They would never believe him.

"We thought you'd be pleased," said Dad.

Faced with the children's strange concern for an old bear's head, his high spirits were slipping away. He shook his head. He would never understand children.

"We'll make money, lots of money. More people will come when we've redecorated. We'll be rich," said Ian's mum.

44

"I don't want to be rich. I want Rosa," Rachel muttered quietly.

"But it's all arranged. You'll love it, really you will. You'll see."

"Couldn't we just keep the bear's head, Dad?" asked Ian. "Please."

"No!" Dad was feeling angry now. "We'll be able to buy all sorts of things when we really make money. We won't make money without redecorating. That bear's head has to go, and that's that." He got up from his chair and walked out of the kitchen.

"Mum."

"No, Ian. Go and play somewhere with Rachel so I can get on."

Yet later, when they told Rosa, all she said was, "Then you must be quick."

"But what if we don't get the herbs and can't find a crystal? You won't be able to turn back into a real person and they'll throw you in the skip. We'll never see you again," whispered Ian.

When Rachel started crying Rosa picked them up and sat them on her knees as she had when Rachel had first met her.

"Dry your eyes, nina. Listen, I am not dead yet. We have six weeks. That is a long time. I have waited for so many years. I have learnt to be patient. You will find those things that I need. If not, then we will think of something else. I have faith that you will do your best. What more could a bear ask for."

She held them close. Her strong arms crushed them into her sweet smelling fur. Her slow, strong, heartbeat made them feel so safe and sure; they quite forgot to be miserable.

Rosa was so solid, so real. Even though the pale light of dawn was just beginning to show through the high front windows of the restaurant, Rosa was still there, the magic still worked. It made them feel that they could succeed. She needed their help. They had to save Rosa.

Chapter 7

The start of school pushed all thoughts of Rosa out of their minds: if only for a short time. The first two days passed in slow confusion. There was so much to remember and learn; new school, new classes, new teachers and hopefully, new friends.

Saturday came, yet they were still no closer to finding the herb or a crystal. Workers were beginning to turn up to talk with their parents and plans were being made for the restaurant.

Rachel and Ian visited Rosa, saying very little. She must have seen the strange people and understood why they were there. The children didn't stay long. School was leaving them tired, with early nights being demanded by their parents.

Only three weeks to go before the work started now. A big red circle was drawn around the start date on the calendar in the kitchen. The work would start on the Friday and would take all week. It was supposed to be finished by the following Monday in time for the new furniture.

The only good news was that Ian was going to the

football trial. He hadn't really wanted to. How could he play football with Rosa in such danger?

Lots of the boys in Ian's class played football at break time and Darren, who was asked to look after Ian on the first day, got him to join in with their games in the playground. They all agreed Ian was a good player and must go to the try out. How could he say no? They were all so friendly.

Football was allowed in the junior playground every break time, including dinner play. The rest of the boys who didn't like football and the girls (whether they wanted to join in with the football or not) were pushed to the edge of the playground.

Ian didn't mind this, but when he told Rachel, she said at once that it wasn't fair. Why should the boys have all the space? Boys were so horrid sometimes, nasty and cruel. Ian laughed, but he would remember her words the next wet dinner playtime.

The dinner ladies had taken away the sponge ball the boys were kicking around the classroom and told them to play quietly. Feeling bored, Darren found an old game of Ghosts in the wet play cupboard. They looked at the battered box. Were all the bits there?

"D'you want to play?" asked Darren, looking at all the boys standing around him.

"Ghosts? There's no such thing," Paul sneered.

"Yes there is. I saw it on telly," replied Marcus.

48

"That's just tricks," said Irwin.

"But it showed you. There was witches too."

"Yeah, well, my dad said it's all a load of rubbish. It's all made up."

"There is witches," shouted Marcus. "I've seen them. They can do tricks and magic and things."

"Oh yeah! I bet. My dad said anyone who believes in magic is stupid," shouted Paul.

"Yeah? Well I do and I'm not stupid, so why don't you just shut up, Paul."

"Who's going to make me?"

"I will, if you don't shut up," Marcus shouted. He was standing very close to Paul and had gone very red.

Suddenly Paul reached out to grab Marcus. It was then that Ian did something really stupid. Before he could stop himself he had shouted out.

"Leave him alone! Marcus is right."

"How d'you know, new boy?"

"Because I've seen magic."

"Yeah? Where? On telly."

Paul was shouting now, in a horrid taunting voice.

"No!" shouted Ian. "In real life. The bear's head in our restaurant comes alive, so there."

The boys were staring at him. He looked back at each of their disbelieving faces. Even Marcus was looking at him strangely.

Oh no! Why had he said that? He shouldn't have told them. What if they believed him? There was no chance of that by the look on their faces. Why did he have to say that? Why had he joined in?

There was a sudden laugh from Irwin.

"In your restaurant? Ha, ha. A bear that comes alive? You are stupid."

"He's a loony, he's a loony," shrieked Asif.

In a moment they were all saying it, laughing and pointing at him. Marcus was forgotten now.

What could he say? They didn't believe him, even though he knew it was true. But he should never, ever have said anything.

Just then the dinner lady came in, calling for the school dinners and packed lunches to line up. They left him standing on the carpet and rushed off, pushing to be first in the queue. There was a prickle of tears in his eyes as he joined the line.

"You shouldn't tell them things like that. They're the ones who are stupid. They don't know nothin'."

Ian turned.

There standing behind him was Serafina, the tallest girl in class: dark brown skin, hair in tight braids that went right over her head and hung down her back.

"My Mum says boys who play football don't have nothin' else going on in their silly heads. Just like my brothers." Serafina grinned, her whole face lighting up with affection for the stupidity of boys.

Ian couldn't resist smiling back.

"I play football," he said.

"Yes, but you're different. I didn't know you lived in a restaurant. Have you really got a bear in it?"

Ian hesitated. He stared at her for a moment, taking in the tall, slim girl in her smart school uniform of grey trousers and red top. At the confident, relaxed slant of her shoulders, with her head held questioningly to one side. Should he trust this girl? He had only seen her since last week and she hadn't spoken to him before. She didn't even sit on his table.

"Yes, there's a bear's head on the wall."

"How does it come alive then?"

Serafina spoke as if it were the most natural thing in the world for a bear's head to come alive. She was just puzzled as to how it happened, that's all.

Just then the line started moving and Serafina and Ian walked side by side down to the dinner hall.

"Not now. I'll tell you later. When there aren't so many people around."

By the time they had finished their dinner it had stopped raining and they all went outside to play, except for Ian and Serafina. Ian was the first one to volunteer to stay in and tidy away all the wet play toys and games. The dinner lady said they were to hurry. She had to supervise all the other children who were tidying up.

Serafina had looked

at Ian curiously when he had said they would tidy up. She had agreed anyway.

"Aren't you going to tell me, then?" she asked.

"Tell you what?" Ian grinned.

"You know. How your bear comes alive. That's why you said we'd do the tidying up. I'm not stupid, you know." Serafina's very white teeth grinned back at him.

"I didn't want the boys to be around when I told you. They think I'm mad now. How can I play football with them again?" Ian looked miserable.

"Just tell 'em you said the first thing that came into your head to stop them fighting. They'll believe you. They always believe me when I say things like that."

"I hadn't thought of that. Thanks," said Ian.

"That's okay." She paused. "Come on then, tell me or the dinner lady will be back. We'd better tidy up as well or she'll tell us off."

He knew he'd have to tell her in the end and he knew that she would believe him straight away. So, as they picked up the toys, Ian explained about coming to live in the restaurant. When he got to the bit about Rosa first coming alive she stopped and stared at him.

"Wow!" she said. "I wish I'd been there. Can I come and see Rosa?"

Ian stopped.

"I'll ask my Mum if you can come round after school. Do you know where *The Bear* restaurant is?"

"Is it the one up on the high street?" she asked.

"That's it," replied Ian.

"I go home part of that way. We could walk together

if you like."

"Okay. I have to collect my little sister from the Infants first and we have to go straight home or my Mum worries. She doesn't want to leave the restaurant. She says I'm old enough to bring Rachel home on my own now, but we mustn't be late"

Just then the dinner lady came in and told them to go out and play. They got their coats and went out into the rapidly drying playground. Darren saw them and shouted out,

"Come on, Bear, you're on Marcus's side."

Ian laughed. "See you after school." He smiled at Serafina and ran off to play football with the boys.

Chapter 8

Straight after school he told Serafina he'd see her at the front gates and rushed off to Rachel's class to collect her. All the rest of the infants had gone home.

They were on their own.

As Ian started off down the corridor, Rachel pushed him into the cloakroom. She reached into her bag and took something out.

Slowly Rachel unfolded a neat tissue parcel and showed him what was inside it. He stared. There in the middle of the pale pink tissue was a small, pointed, clear quartz crystal.

"Where did you get that from?" he asked.

Rachel looked away.

"I just got it," she said. "It's a crystal. Miss Winter said that people used them a long time ago to do magic. So we can use it to do the magic and turn Rosa into a lady again."

"Yes, but where did you get it from? You didn't steal it, did you?" he accused her.

"No, I've only borrowed it. We can give it back when we've turned Rosa into a lady again." Rachel's face had gone quite pink.

"You've taken it from your classroom haven't you? You have stolen it. Oh, Rachel! How could you? Stealing is wrong. You know that. Mum and Dad would be really angry if they knew. So would Rosa if I told her where you got it. Oh you are stupid!"

"No I'm not," Rachel's voice was loud and she was very red now. "Rosa needs it. She won't mind. You're just being horrid because you didn't think of it first." Tears started to trickle down her cheeks.

Just then the big shape of the caretaker, his broom and black dustbin bag in hand, came into the cloakroom.

"Everything all right?" his loud voice boomed out.

"Yes thanks," said Ian

Quickly Rachel folded the tissue over the crystal and shoved it into her pocket.

"Come on, Rachel. Serafina's waiting for us."

He started to hurry down the corridor, dragging Rachel behind him.

"Slow down, Ian, don't go so fast," protested Rachel. "Who's Serafina?"

"She's a girl I met in my class. I had to tell her about Rosa. She's going to come round after school to see her."

"Today?"

"I don't know. She's got to ask her mum and then I'll have to ask ours: so I don't know yet. She's waiting at the Junior School gates. Hurry up or she'll go without us."

They ran across the infant playground and went around the corner of the junior building. Had Serafina waited? Oh yes, she had. They raced across to the gates.

"Rachel's stolen a crystal from her class," Ian was cross and out of breath. Rachel went red again.

"No, I haven't," she replied stubbornly. "I've only borrowed it. We need it. You're being mean to me."

Rachel started crying. Ian pulled her along and explained to Serafina about the crystal. Serafina stopped.

"Wait a minute, Ian. Can I have a look, Rachel?" she said with a big soothing smile. "Oh, it's beautiful, isn't it? Why did you take it, Rachel?"

"They're going to throw Rosa away when they start decorating the restaurant and Rosa needs a crystal and lots of other things to do her magic to turn herself back into a lady and we've only got three weeks left and they'll put her in the skip and we'll never see her again and I love Rosa and I don't want her to be thrown away."

Rachel looked so sad after this long tearful outburst that Serafina pulled her into her arms and cuddled her.

After a little while she stopped crying. Serafina crouched down in front of her and holding her at arm's length, looked straight into her red-rimmed eyes.

"Can I tell you something, Rachel?" she asked.

"What?" said Rachel, staring back?

"You do want to help Rosa, don't you?"

Rachel nodded.

"Well, tomorrow you can take this crystal back and tell your teacher you took it by mistake." Then as Rachel started to protest she quickly went on. "Because my mum's got crystals at home just like that one, only bigger. She sells them to people. She runs a shop with my Aunty Eileen. If you want I'll ask my mum if I can borrow one and then we can use it to save Rosa. Would you like that?" Rachel nodded. "Then dry your eyes and we'll walk home and ask her. She always says yes 'cos she knows I look after them. You'd better not tell her what it's for though, or she might not lend it to me. Come on."

Ian stared in amazement at Serafina. How had she managed to calm Rachel so easily and quickly? Ian was used to having arguments with Rachel. Ever since he'd burnt her doll, he'd been treating her as his irritating little sister.

Serafina had worked a miracle!

She took Rachel's hand and they walked along the pavement. After a while Serafina started singing a song they'd learnt at school and Rachel and Ian joined in

"*We all live in a Yellow Submarine*," they sang.

When she didn't know the words Serafina made them up, and then they all laughed because her new words were so silly. Ian felt really pleased he'd told Serafina about Rosa. She had sorted Rachel out so well. Much better than anything he could have done.

They soon got to Serafina's house. It was different from the rest of the houses in the street. It was made out of yellow and grey bricks instead of dull red and it was bigger. It had an enormous garden too.

Serafina told them it used to be a farmhouse and when they built the other houses on the farmland they had left the farmhouse in the middle.

Serafina's mum was a tall lady, big and graceful, with the same smile as Serafina, but her hair was long and loose and it curled around her face and bounced about her shoulders.

Did she mind if Serafina went round to their house to play? Of course not, but Serafina was to be back by six for her tea. Yes, she could borrow a crystal, so long as she was sure she would look after it. It was surprisingly easy.

"Your mum let you have the crystal so easily," said Ian as they walked along the street.

"My mum trusts me. She knows I'll be good 'cos I always am," said Serafina, cradling the new crystal in her hands. She had wrapped it in a shiny blue cloth and was holding it very carefully.

Soon they could see the restaurant in the distance, at the other end of the high street.

"If you're not allowed into the restaurant when it's open, how will I get to see Rosa?" said Serafina.

"It's shut now. It closes after serving lunches, and then it opens again at 7:30. We'll sneak in when Mum and Dad aren't looking," replied Ian.

He took them along the road that led to the rear entrance of the restaurant. The road ended beside a fence with a gate, which Ian opened with a key.

You couldn't go through the alleyway door because it locked from the inside, unless you clicked the lock down so it wouldn't shut. He'd done that when he went through the alleyway to check Rosa's photograph when all this had started.

That seemed so long ago now, but it was only a few weeks. They went inside and Ian shouted, "Mum!"

"Yes dear, I'm upstairs."

"Come on Serafina." They ran up the stairs to the kitchen. "Mum, can Serafina come round and play?"

Ian's mum turned and smiled at Serafina. "Of course she can. It's nice to meet Ian's friends. He hasn't brought anyone home since we've been here. Where do you live?"

"In Frampton Road. It's near the new houses on the way to school," replied Serafina.

"Would you all like a drink and something to eat?" asked Mum.

"Yes please," they chorused.

"Where are you going to be?" she asked.

"In my room," said Ian quickly, before Rachel could speak. "We might go in the garden after," he added.

"Right," said Mum and she went off towards the kitchen. Ian led Serafina to his bedroom.

It wasn't big. The bed, wardrobe and his floor-to-ceiling open shelf storage system, with its neatly arranged, multicoloured plastic boxes, took up a lot of the room, but it had a small green armchair as well as a beanbag seat with footballers printed on it.

Ian sat on the bed. Rachel jumped onto the beanbag and wriggled about, getting comfortable.

Serafina sank into the little armchair. It had a high back with low sides and the seat was close to the floor. Serafina's knees stuck up because she was so tall. It made her look strange, as if she had shrunk and only had a little body.

She looked around Ian's room, with its plain white walls and swirly green and brown carpet.

"How d'you keep your bedroom so neat, Ian?" she

asked. Ian shrugged. Having a super organised mother meant he didn't really have much choice.

"Mum'd only moan if I didn't."

Serafina shook her head in wonder. What would Ian's mum make of her higgledy-piggledy mess?

"Can I see the crystal again, Serafina?" asked Rachel.

"Better wait until after your mum brings the drinks and things. We don't want her to see it, do we?"

Serafina acted a bit like a mum to Rachel, thought Ian. That might be because she had younger brothers. She was much better than he was at getting Rachel to do what she wanted. Perhaps if he bought Rachel a new doll they might be friends again.

"When can I see Rosa?" Serafina asked.

"After we've had our snacks. If we rush down straight away Mum might get suspicious. We can say we're going to the garden and then look in the restaurant as we go."

Ian still found it hard to accept that Serafina had believed him. He knew she did. It was just that every now and then he found it difficult to believe it himself. Serafina seemed to think it was quite normal for a bear's head to come alive.

Serafina looked around the room.

"Can I play on your Xbox, Ian?" she asked.

"Okay. Have you got one at home?"

"No. My brother lets me play on his sometimes. He hasn't got many games I like though. What have you got?" asked Serafina.

For answer Ian opened a cupboard door in his shelf system. On the shelf inside was a massive pile of computer games.

"Wow! That's brilliant." Serafina started to look through the games.

"All his games are about fighting and killing and things like that." Rachel made a horrible face at him. Her voice had that nasty, sneering *I'm better than you are* sound to it.

"So what?" Ian stood up quickly. His voice was loud and sharp as he stood over her. "They're better than your silly games about cats and dogs."

He was angry with her again. She always made fun of what he liked. He was going to shout at her when a squeal of delight came from Serafina.

She was still looking at the computer games and seemed to be ignoring their quarrel.

"Can I play this one?" she asked, with a smile, waving a game in the air. "D'you want to play with me, Rachel?"

Before Rachel could reply there was a sudden knock at the door and Ian's mum came in carrying a tray loaded with glasses, lemonade, biscuits, crisps and three apples.

"Thanks, Mum," said Ian and Rachel together.

"Thank you," said Serafina.

"That's all right. Bring the tray to the kitchen when you've finished please Ian," said Mum as she went out and shut the door.

They attacked the refreshments. Serafina sat down at the screen with a glass of lemonade and a packet of crisps. She started the game.

Ian and Rachel watched as Serafina expertly collected treasure with her character.

"Are you going to play with me, Rachel? You have to get enough to pay the ransom so you can get the people out of the castle," explained Serafina as Rachel sat down beside her.

Ian had forgotten about this game. It was almost the first game he'd had. Uncle Grant had bought it for him. He'd really liked it for a while. It was only when he got others that he'd stopped playing it.

Rachel and Serafina were having lots of fun, he thought, as he munched his biscuits and drank the lemonade. He felt left out. Serafina was his friend and she wasn't even playing with him. Rachel always spoiled things. First it was Rosa, now Serafina, and they still hadn't helped Rosa.

"Rachel! You've got to take the school crystal back tomorrow."

"I know. I will," said Rachel, still concentrating on the computer game.

"Where is it?"

"What do you want to know for?"

"If you get caught before you put it back you'll be in trouble and they'll tell Mum and Dad you've been stealing, and they're going to ask why you took it and that's going to make it hard to save Rosa. So where is it? I want to see it?" Ian was almost shouting again.

Serafina looked at him strangely.

"Ian's right, Rachel. You can keep my crystal to show to Rosa tonight. I'd better have it back tomorrow just in case my mum wonders where it is."

"Can I have another look now?" asked Rachel.

Serafina took the wrapped crystal out of her pocket. Carefully she opened the cloth and held the crystal up for Rachel to see.

It was beautiful. About eight centimetres long, it had six sides, like a pencil. Not the rounded ones, the other sort, a hexagonal prism.

It was clear as glass at the pointed end. The other end looked as if it had been broken from rock. There were still some small pieces stuck to it.

It was the inside that was different. As Serafina held it up to the light from the window and turned it between her thumb and first finger, what looked like flat cracks glittered and sparkled in fantastic shapes.

Deeper inside where the light caught it, shining rainbows appeared and disappeared. The late evening sun from the window gave it a golden orange glint. There was a magical feeling in the air. With this crystal Rosa could do anything.

"Oh!" said Rachel. "It's lovely. Can I hold it?"

"Yes," said Serafina.

"No," said Ian, both at the same time.

"Why not?" demanded Rachel.

"You'll break it or something," Ian spoke quietly.

He knew that he had broken the magical moment. The sun went behind a cloud. It no longer gave the crystal its sparkle.

"You're just like Mum. She never lets me do things," Rachel's eyes filled with tears.

"Hold it gently then," whispered Serafina as shadows crept into the room.

"Oh thank you, Serafina. You're my best friend."

Ian stood in the dark. Only the computer screen gave light to the room. Why did he feel that Rachel was stealing everything from him? She made him so angry. How could Serafina do this to him? She was supposed to be his friend.

Rachel turned the crystal over and over, trying to see the rainbow again. "Can I keep it in my room, Serafina, please can I? It's so lovely,"

Ian smiled to himself. This would stop Rachel getting her way again. Serafina would have to say no. She'd already said her mum wanted it back safely. Her answer must be no.

But instead Serafina smiled, saying. "Okay, just make sure you look after it properly. You will, won't you?" Rachel smiled a big smile and nodded vigorously.

"You mustn't drop it, either," she continued, "Mum says they don't like being dropped."

Ian stared at her in astonishment. All thoughts of Rachel were swept away. He almost said, "How can it mind being dropped? It's only a bit of rock." It was a very beautiful rock, of course, but still a rock.

Suddenly another thought popped into his head. If a bear's head could come alive then perhaps a rock could have feelings. He was asking Serafina to believe in a magic bear that was really a person. A few weeks ago he would never have believed that either if someone had told him. So he didn't say anything.

A sudden knock at the door made them all jump guiltily. Serafina tried to grab the crystal. Rachel was

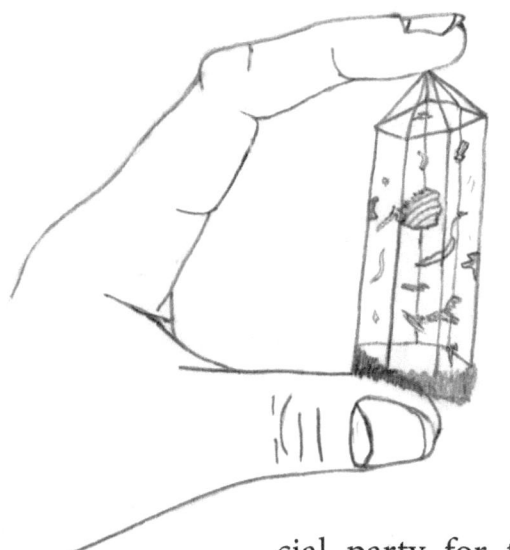

quicker. She had quietly slipped it into her pocket and sat down at the computer. Serafina joined her.

Ian went to the door as it opened. It was Mum. He listened with a pounding heart as she explained.

"Ian, the special party for tonight have just phoned. They're going to be early and the staff isn't here yet. I'll have to go down now. I've put your tea out on the table. All you have to do is turn the oven on for the pizza. Is Serafina going to stay?"

Mum smiled at Serafina.

"I don't know. I'll have to phone my mum. She said to be back for tea by six o'clock."

"There's enough there for you if you can stay. Be good. See you later."

The door closed. They looked at each other.

"Can I phone my mum?" asked Serafina.

"Haven't you got a mobile?"

"No, I wanted one, but my mum says they heat up your brain and they aren't good for children. She won't let me have one till I'm older. Have you got one?"

"No, I wanted a camera phone. Mum said I have to wait till my next birthday. Come on, I'll show you where the phone is."

Ian opened the door and took Serafina along to the big kitchen. He gave her the phone. There on the table was their tea. Ian looked at it and then went back to his room. Rachel was gone. Ian went to her room and opened the door.

"Rachel, where's the crystal?" he demanded

"What do you want to know for? Serafina said that I could keep it."

"Only for tonight when we show it to Rosa. What have you done with it?" Ian's voice was getting louder.

"Stop shouting at me. I've got it hidden. I'll bring it with me tonight. Go away. I want to be on my own."

Rachel walked towards him, almost pushing him out of her room. She slammed the door behind him. Ian stood there, angry again.

With a sigh he went back to the kitchen. Helping Rosa seemed to make things so complicated. He could hear Serafina talking, as he got closer. She put the telephone down just as he arrived.

"I've got to go. Mum's going out. My big brother's got football training, so I have to look after the twins till Dad gets home. Can I see Rosa before I go?" she asked.

"I think Mum's down there. We'll have to pretend you've come to say goodbye."

He walked down the stairs with her, past the dark wooden panels in the hall and through to the restaurant. Mum wasn't there. Perhaps she was in the restaurant kitchen, thought Ian. Serafina stopped and stared at Rosa across the tables.

"When does she come alive?" she whispered.

"At night. The magic doesn't work in the day. She can still hear and see though, come on."

They walked over and stood in front of Rosa. There seemed to be a smile somewhere in her fierce gaze.

"Serafina's going to help us, Rosa. She's brought a crystal with her. Rachel's got it. We'll come and see you tonight." Ian was whispering now. It seemed the right thing to do.

"How can I meet her if she only comes alive at night?" whispered Serafina.

"I dunno," Ian whispered back.

There was a sudden noise of footsteps entering the restaurant behind them.

"What are you doing in here, Ian? You know Dad doesn't like it." Mum had come back from the kitchen carrying a great pile of plates.

"He was just showing me the bear, Mrs. Johnson. I'd better go now. Thank you for having me," Serafina smiled at Ian's mum, turned and began to walk back to the entrance. Ian followed her.

Outside the restaurant, Serafina looked at Ian.

"See you at school tomorrow. Tell Rachel goodbye from me. Don't worry about the crystal, Ian; I know she'll look after it." Ian turned and walked indoors.

Chapter 9

Rosa thought the crystal was marvellous. She said she could feel the energy coming through it. She was very funny that night. She did headstands and rolled over and over, laughing in a bubbly way that shook her whole body.

They played chasing games with Rosa running after them round and round the tables. They laughed and giggled for ages.

"Oh, ninos! This crystal makes me feel so young again. When can I meet this lovely Serafina?"

Rosa was so happy. It was only when Ian said he still hadn't found the Spanish herb that she stopped.

"I'll try to go online at school and see what I can find on the web." He'd tried to explain about computers and the internet to her before. A sad look came across her face and she sent them off to bed with instructions for them to look everywhere.

After they had said goodnight, had a last bear hug and crept off to beds grown cold, Rosa went over to the window and looked out at the rain that had begun to fall. She sat looking outside for a long while. The happy

Rosa had gone. A worried look had taken its place. A pale tear trickled down beside her nose. Even when she'd wiped it away with her paw another and another soon replaced it.

If Ian and Rachel had been there they would have known why. Despite her joy in the crystal she was still sad and worried. If Ian didn't find the herb soon the painters would come to redecorate the Restaurant. They would throw her away and she would never turn back into a real person.

The dark pouring rain turned pale grey in the cloud-hidden dawn. Rosa walked back to where her shield hung on its great hooks. With a last look around she slid up onto it leaving only a damp patch on the windowsill where her wet paw had been.

It was not until the following week that things started to happen. The children had talked a lot about Rosa. Now that they had the crystal, all that was left was to find the Spanish herb.

The only thing they could think of to do was to visit the local library and see if they had any books about herbs. Serafina said they should use the library computers to go on the internet and search. It was really hard for her to go online at home. Her brother Micah was always on it for his schoolwork and it was in her mum's office anyway. She didn't want anyone asking awkward questions. As Ian's parents hadn't had it installed yet, what else could they do?

Serafina suggested they go on Saturday because she often had to baby-sit while her mum went out on business after school. They could pretend they were doing research for homework or something. She asked again about seeing Rosa, but Ian had plenty of other things to think about.

He had gone to the football trial after school on Thursday and had been on good form in the first half, yet it was only when Miss Dennis let him go in defence that he played really well.

He was a good defender. It was hard to get past him. He always seemed to be there at the right moment, jockeying the attackers until the rest of the defence rushed back. He marked the key players just the way he had been taught at his last school by Mr. Merton.

He had a brilliant second half and stopped two goals on his own. Miss Dennis said she'd post the team-list for their first game in the morning.

Ian couldn't wait for school next day. When he got there and pushed his way through the crowd of boys, he saw his name printed out as centre back. The match was next week, on Wednesday after school. They were to play away and would travel there in the school minibus.

He was so pleased that he played football all day at every playtime, quite forgetting he had promised to talk to Serafina about Rosa.

In the excitement somehow Rosa was pushed to the edge of his mind. He knew they had to save Rosa, but this was his first match in the school team. They couldn't do anything else about Rosa until Saturday. This was important too. Didn't Serafina understand? Serafina said he didn't seem to care about Rosa any more. They only had ten more days to save her.

What could he do? They were going to the library on Saturday. He did care, but he was in the team.

"That's the trouble with you boys, you only think about football," said Serafina. "You've got nothing else in your heads. I thought you were going to be different." Now they were both shouting.

Suddenly Rachel started crying. She shouted at them both, telling them how selfish they were. Rosa was going to be thrown away and would never get to be a real person again.

They looked at each other. How had this happened? Ian felt guilty for only thinking about himself. Serafina wished she hadn't shouted and Rachel was just miserable. They walked home in silence.

The rest of the week seemed to go so slowly. They didn't say sorry to each other, they just knew they were. Ian could hardly think about the football match and he felt so miserable that he and Rachel didn't even visit Rosa for two days.

Saturday came. They had arranged to meet Serafina outside the restaurant at ten o'clock. By half past ten she had still not arrived. They walked slowly round to her house, trying to believe that she was only late and that nothing was seriously wrong.

Her mum answered the door. Serafina was ill. She

had been sick all night and could not come out. Her mum hoped she would be better tomorrow and would see them at school on Monday.

What could they do? Serafina had been going to use her library card. They hadn't joined yet. You couldn't exactly ask to use someone's library card when they were ill, so they walked home again.

There was no way that Mum or Dad would come with them to join. Saturday was the restaurant's busiest day. They would have to wait until Monday.

Serafina didn't come to school on Monday though. When they knocked on the way home to find out what was wrong, her mum said she had something called gastro-enteritis: a tummy bug. That meant she wouldn't be back to school for at least a week. Rosa would be thrown away by then. What were they going to do? The library had been their last hope.

When they told Rosa, she said she would try the magic without the herb. She wasn't sure if it would be successful. She thought it might work. Anyway they were not to worry. They would think of something. Yet they knew she was just being cheerful and didn't really believe it.

Tuesday came. Mum said they had to be careful in the corridor when they came home from school. Dad wanted the wooden panelling in the corridor taken away because it was so dark and old-fashioned. Then they would decorate. He knew the customers didn't see this area, but he did. They were starting in the corridor today and moving on to do the same in the restaurant next week.

It was when they got back from school and saw what the workmen had done, that Ian had his brilliant idea.

They walked in as usual. The decorators had just finished. Where the panelling had been in the corridor was bare plaster, except at the end where, past the doors to the kitchen and the restaurant, was an old-fashioned wooden door with a key in a big metal lock.

When Ian asked, Dad said it was a cellar. No one had known it was there. There was nothing much down there, just some old junk. When they could afford it, Dad wanted to turn it into a wine cellar. They were not to go down there, Dad would show it to them when he had time. There was nothing much to see anyway, just piles of old rubbish.

Suddenly Ian knew what to do. The cellar; they would put Rosa down the cellar. They could hide her there on Sunday, the night before the decorators came. Dad would think the workmen had thrown her in the skip.

It was a brilliant idea. She could stay there until they had found her Spanish herb and she could magic herself human again.

Ian was very pleased with himself. Even better, he was in the team for the match tomorrow. He was so excited he just couldn't wait.

Chapter 10

Serafina would be amazed. Ian had to tell her. He would call in on his way home and wouldn't stay for long, even though his mum knew he was going to be late home from school after the football match. It was getting dark and Ian didn't want to walk home in the dark.

Not that he was worried about the dark of course. It was just that Mum had said to walk straight home after the match. If he was late she would be angry and she might not let him go again.

Serafina's mum answered the door. She gave him a smile of recognition and invited him in. Yes, Serafina was better, but the doctor had said it would take time to get her strength back, so she wasn't allowed up yet.

Ian was shown upstairs by the little twins, who kept giggling at each other and muttering about boyfriends.

Serafina was lying in bed; comics, books, paper and pens scattered around her, which only added to the general state of untidiness. Serafina was right; her room was a real mess.

"Ian! Did you win?"

"No, we lost four two."

Ian was smiling at her.

"You lost?" Serafina looked puzzled. Why was he so cheerful if they had lost?

"We were doing great in the first half, two one up. Then Asif fell over the ball and hurt his leg. We didn't stand a chance then. But that's not what I came to tell you. You know we were playing against St. Peter's?"

Serafina nodded.

"Well, their pitch is right next door to the church. They scored three times: you should have seen their strikers. I went to get the ball for a goal kick after it went in the graveyard. And there it was. I couldn't believe it. I'd almost given up hope and there it was," Ian stopped. He was out of breath with excitement.

"Ian, what are you talking about? What was in the graveyard?"

"The herb! The herb! Rosa's herb. It was growing there. A great big bit of it growing in a bunch. I recognised it from my drawing." Ian was grinning happily.

"Oh, Ian! Have you got some? Can I see it?" Serafina wriggled in her bed in excitement.

"I couldn't pick it, could I? I had my football kit on. The team would have thought I was crazy. We'll have to go and get some later. When you're better."

"Mum said I've got to wait 'til Monday, then I can go back to school. I thought you said the decorators were going to start then. They'll put Rosa in the skip."

Serafina's smile had gone. She looked worried and very tired.

Ian smiled. "Well, that's just where you're wrong, Serafina." He told her about the cellar and his plan and he was right, she did think it was brilliant.

With Rosa in the cellar they would have time to go to St. Peter's church and get the herb they wanted. All they had to do then was to collect all the other bits together and Rosa could be human again. It really was a brilliant idea. Except that wasn't quite how it turned out.

Chapter 11

It was on Sunday night, after the restaurant had closed and his parents were safely in bed, that Ian went downstairs to Rosa.

She was waiting. Ian had told her about getting the herb and hiding her from the decorators in the cellar. Tomorrow they started work in the restaurant. Rosa must go into the cellar tonight.

Rosa wanted to know where Rachel was.

Ian was ready for this one. He didn't want Rachel around spoiling his idea. He was going to do this on his own. He hadn't told her he was coming downstairs. She was still asleep in bed. Of course, he'd had to tell her about his plan. Otherwise she would still think Rosa would be thrown away and who knows what she might have done then.

He'd had to tell her. That didn't mean he had to let her help him though. So he said to Rosa that Rachel was too tired and was fast asleep. Rosa looked at him strangely. She knows, thought Ian, but Rosa didn't say anything. Getting her into the cellar was too important for her to make a fuss.

Together they looked at her shield. Somehow they had to lift it off the big metal hooks that held it up above the pretend fireplace. It looked heavy.

Rosa stretched up to try and reach it.

"It's no good, Ian, it's too high. I cannot touch it."

"Let me get on your shoulders, Rosa. I might be able to reach it then."

Rosa bent down and Ian climbed up onto her shoulders: one leg dangling on either side of her huge neck. Slowly, carefully, so as not to knock Ian off, Rosa straightened up to her full height. Leaning forward against the wall, Rosa steadied herself. Ian reached out towards the shield.

It *was* heavy. Would he be able to lift it?

He pushed it up slightly, pulling it towards him, lifting at the same time, trying to get it off the curved hooks. It was difficult. One end moved very slightly, the weight of the wood holding it down on the hook. Rosa shifted beneath him.

"Careful, Rosa," he warned. He looked at the shield and thought. It had to come off both hooks at once. Could he do it? No, it was too heavy for him to lift on his own. Wait a minute, yes, he had it.

"Rosa, can you push me up higher?"

"I will try, ninito."

Stretching, Rosa boosted him up a little higher. Holding onto the bottom of the shield, Ian suddenly found it slipping over the hooks as Rosa pushed him higher.

He almost toppled backwards off Rosa's shoulders

with the weight of it. Luckily the shield slipped forward, resting on Rosa's head, and he regained his balance.

"I've got it!"

"Well done, ninito,"

Rosa took a step backwards. Ian wobbled again, clutching at the moving shield. Rosa growled as it scraped painfully over her right ear. She sat down suddenly. Ian grabbed at her head; the shield slipped from his grasp and fell down to the carpet with a dull thud. It was done.

"We did it, Rosa, we did it," Ian almost shouted out loud in his delight.

Rosa rolled over onto her back, stretching out her paws and wriggling her toes.

"I am glad you had this clever thought, Ian."

"We're not done yet, Rosa. We need to take your shield down into the cellar, so you can be out of the way when the decorators start tomorrow."

"Can you carry it Ian?"

Carefully moving one corner of the shield, he found he could just about lift it. Rosa couldn't do it; she'd over-balance on her hind legs. He'd have to do it himself

"Yes. It's quite a weight though," he walked a few paces, struggling not to drop it.

"Ian, you rest it on my shoulders to make it easy."

Ian manoeuvred the shield so it was resting on Rosa's back. He had to hold it there to keep it from falling off, because every step Rosa took made it wobble.

It was easier this way than trying to do it all on his own, even though it was difficult going in and out of the closely packed tables. With Ian walking by her side, holding the shield on, they made their way slowly through the restaurant, stopping frequently.

At last they reached the door to the corridor. Carefully they turned left, towards the cellar door. The key in the lock was stiff; it had not been used for ages. Ian moved it backwards and forwards.

Nothing happened.

He tried again.

That was better. With a grinding sound the key turned in the rusty lock. Ian pulled at the handle. The door opened with creaking hinges. There was enough light to show steps leading down into blackness. Ian turned and began lifting the shield off Rosa's back.

A sudden noise made him look beyond Rosa, to the top of the stairs. Standing there in her dressing gown, looking incredibly angry, was Rachel.

"Ian! You went without me," Rachel spoke angrily, only just managing not to shout. Ian stood there guiltily, saying nothing.

What could he say? That she was too silly and noisy? He didn't want her hanging around? He didn't like her? She was always so nasty to him?

He tried to think of some way to stop her being angry, wishing Serafina were here. Serafina always knew what to do about Rachel.

Then Rachel was running down the stairs towards them, her dressing gown flapping around her legs. Suddenly Rachel screamed and was *falling* down the stairs towards them, her dressing gown wrapped around her legs. Rosa jumped towards Rachel. Holding the shield on his own made Ian stagger backwards towards the cellar steps.

Rosa reached the bottom of the stairs at the same time as Rachel. They lay there together for a moment in stunned silence, before Rachel started crying.

Rosa cuddled her, murmuring words in Spanish, to try and comfort her, but Rachel got louder and louder.

From upstairs there was the sound of a door flung open, the light clicking on and Dad's voice shouting.

"What's happening? Who's there?"

"Rosa! On your shield, quick,"

Ian's voice cut across the noise of Rachel's sobs. Rosa looked up, stared at Ian, said something to Rachel in Spanish, and raced back towards Ian. There was the strange watery sound as she flowed towards the shield. Then she was there, back in her place.

Ian staggered; the extra weight of Rosa's head over-balanced him. He tottered backwards, towards the cellar, slipped on the carpet and dropped Rosa, who crashed on to the top step and disappeared into the blackness.

Ian could hear her bumping down the cellar steps. There was a muffled thump as she reached the bottom.

The only sound now was Rachel's sobs.

Their father appeared at the top of the stairs. He stared at them. Then understanding seemed to dawn on him.

"I thought I told you not to go down that cellar."

Rushing down the stairs he strode to the cellar door. He slammed it shut, locked it and put the key in his pocket.

Walking past Ian, who still stood frozen to the spot, he gently picked up Rachel, who had stopped crying, she wasn't really hurt, just bruised.

He said only one word to Ian. "Bed."

As Ian walked upstairs behind dad all he could think about was poor Rosa down in the cold dark cellar. It was all Rachel's fault.

How was he going to get Rosa out from behind the locked cellar door without the key?

Chapter 12

Dad had been very angry with him. Didn't Ian understand Rachel could have been badly hurt? He was old enough not to be so stupid. They expected him to be more responsible. If he'd wanted to look down the cellar why hadn't he asked them if he could?

Dad had gone on and on about it.

There was worse to come. When Ian went downstairs he found the decorators had piled all their equipment, tools and materials in front of the cellar door.

Now he couldn't even talk to Rosa until the decorators had finished. It was a very difficult week. He was on his best behaviour, trying to be as helpful as he could around the flat, to show that they could trust him to be sensible.

The only good thing was that Serafina was well again and had come back to school. Together they worked out how they were going to get the herb from the graveyard at St. Peters church. Ian would ask his mum and dad if he could go to Serafina's house on Saturday for the day. He was sure they would say yes, especially with the decorators working at the weekend to try and get the restaurant finished for when the new furniture arrived on Monday.

They would be glad to have him out of the way.

"Rachel must come too," said Serafina.

"But it was her fault Rosa got locked in the cellar!"

"Yes, I know. But I think it would be much better to have her with us. I don't want to keep wondering what she's doing in your house on her own."

"Oh, okay."

"Why you have to be so horrible to each other I don't know. It's about time you thought about Rosa and not yourselves."

Ian had to admit that she was right, even though he didn't really want Rachel there.

They would go round early and then Serafina would say they were going on a picnic in the park and could they have some sandwiches please. Serafina knew her mother would say yes; and she was right, she did.

Once they were out of the house they went straight to the bus stop. They knew which one it was because Serafina had looked it up on the bus map they had in the bookcase at her house.

None of them said much on the journey. Rachel still wasn't talking to Ian, despite him letting her come along. Rosa had stopped Rachel hurting herself badly when she fell down the stairs, what she couldn't do was to stop her hurting inside. Ian had left her out. She didn't feel like talking at all. Serafina tried for a while then gave up. She concentrated on looking out of the window.

Bus number 65 dropped them two roads away from St. Peter's Church. They could see the tall green spire of the church towering over the tops of the houses. It was easy for them to walk there from the bus stop.

There was no one to be seen as they slipped inside the gate to the overgrown graveyard, and Ian and Serafina were concentrating so much on finding the herb that they didn't notice Rachel wandering to the other side of the churchyard.

Ian led Serafina round the church to the gate he had gone through to get the football. This was going to be easy. The mid-October sun was shining brightly, casting strong shadows as they bent down around the spot that Ian was excitedly pointing to. They could see the herb growing next to the church wall. It looked exactly like Ian's drawing.

"We only need to take a few leaves. Rosa doesn't need much to turn back," Ian reached down to tear some leaves from the herb.

Suddenly it went dark. Had the sun gone in? They looked up. Standing over them was the tall pale-faced figure of a lady dressed in black. She didn't look very pleased. Her lined face crinkled into a frown. The black hat covering her grey hair bobbed backwards and forwards fiercely.

"What do you think you're doing?" she said, pointing an accusing finger at them. "You leave my herbs alone. I grew them from seed myself. If you don't clear off I'll get the vicar to call the police. Where have you come from? I haven't seen you around here before. Was it you who broke the church window? I think we'd better call the police anyway so you can't do any more damage." Before

they could do anything about it she had grabbed their arms and was pulling them towards a small wooden door in the church wall.

Just as they got there, it opened and out walked a smiling Rachel. A young man dressed in a long, black robe followed her.

"Vicar, I've just caught these two young hooligans trying to steal some of my herbs. They probably broke the church window and stole the candlesticks. We'd better call the police." The lady tightened her grip on Ian and Serafina.

"Ian! What have you done?" said Rachel.

"Rachel, is this your brother?" asked the vicar. Rachel nodded. "Then this must be Serafina," he continued. "Mrs. Simpson, this is a misunderstanding. These two children are not the vandals who broke into our church: far from it. They are kind and thoughtful children. Rachel has told me all about their problems."

Ian looked over at Serafina. What had Rachel been telling him?

"It's all right, children. I know all about your poor friend Rosa, from Spain. You see, Mrs. Simpson, their poor friend cannot go back to Spain at the moment and she misses one of the most beautiful herbs in her garden, but she doesn't know its English name, just the Spanish one. Ian here saw the herb in the churchyard when he was playing in the football match the other day, and they wanted to get some of it for their poor homesick friend. What lovely children they are."

Mrs. Simpson hesitated, then smiled and let Ian and

Serafina go.

"Oh, I see, vicar," she said. "Sorry children, I was sure you were up to no good when I saw you. Here, I'll dig you up a side shoot and put it in a pot. You must be very careful with it. It won't like being moved, so it might not grow. It's a powerful herb and it's poisonous too. Wash your hands if you touch it. In the old days it was thought witches used it for magic you know. We call them Christmas Roses. Its proper Latin name is *Hellebore*. I don't know what the Spanish name is."

Fifteen minutes later they were walking back to the bus stop with the herb in a pot, laughing and talking as they went.

Serafina couldn't stop saying how brilliant she thought Rachel was. Even Ian had to agree that Rachel had been wonderful, and what was even better, she had told the truth, well most of it. They had everything that Rosa needed.

All that was left to do now was get her out of the locked cellar.

Chapter 13

It was a very frosty night outside: the first of the autumn. It was still warm in the restaurant, even though all the people had gone. It had been an excellent reopening night. The restaurant had looked wonderful in all its new decorations and the customers had loved the food. Ian's mum and dad were really happy and the best thing was Serafina being allowed to stay overnight.

Serafina would be able to meet Rosa at last, on the very night they were going to release her from the bear spell and set her free.

Persuading Mum and Dad to let her stay had not been easy. The problem, of course, had been the cellar. Dad thinking they were about to explore the cellar without permission made it hard to explain.

Although as Serafina said, "It's better for your parents to think you were exploring the cellar than knowing the real reason."

Ian stood there listening while his Dad went on and on about it. How could he trust them not to do something as stupid again, was what he had said. Ian had to promise faithfully that they would not do anything silly. That was easy. He was definitely not going to do anything silly. Helping Rosa was not silly, so he had promised, knowing he would do nothing wrong.

Then there was more worrying news. Dad wanted the cellar sorted out and the decorators were coming back in two weeks time. The first thing dad had asked them to do was clear out all the junk. That meant Rosa too. After that they were going to decorate. Rosa had to be saved before they started.

It was only that morning that the decorators had removed their equipment, after all the finishing touches were made.

Ian still didn't know if they could get Rosa out of the cellar. He just hoped they could. He had no idea where Dad kept the key. Perhaps Rosa could use her magic somehow and open the door.

Now, all three of them were quietly going down the stairs towards the cellar door, carrier bags full of everything Rosa needed. They couldn't leave her locked in, waiting to be thrown away. Being careful to count the stairs so they wouldn't creak and wake up his parents, they made their way to the cellar door.

Ian whispered into the gap by the lock.

"Rosa! Are you there?" His whisper seemed very loud. There was no answer.

He tried again. "Rosa! It's Ian, and Rachel. We've got everything you wanted and Serafina's here too. Rosa, are you there?" They waited; hearing nothing, except their beating hearts.

Then the sound of claws on wood made them all

90

jump. The unexpected noise seemed to echo around the house. Rosa was there.

"I am here, Ian. What happened? Where have you been all week? I have been so lonely."

"It was the decorators; they left all their stuff piled outside the door. We couldn't get near to it until they had finished."

"Have you the key for the lock?" asked Rosa.

"No I haven't. Dad took it. Can you use your magic to get out?"

"Yes. Move away from the door, ninos."

They moved back, waiting anxiously to see what would happen next.

For a moment there was silence.

The noise started quietly at first, and then quickly became louder. Ian and Rachel recognised the watery sound that Rosa made when she came down from her shield. This time though, it seemed like the sea was in the cellar, rushing towards them.

They listened, wondering what Rosa was doing.

Suddenly a river of dark, liquid fur burst from under the door. It stopped before them, splashing up into the air, churning round and round, gradually settling into the familiar shape of Rosa. The fur stopped moving and, with a sigh, Rosa collapsed into a heap at their feet.

They stood there, looking at her in surprise.

"Oh, Rosa, you are so clever. How did you do that?" Rachel dropped her plastic bag, flung her arms around Rosa's neck and gave her a big hug.

"Be careful Rachel, using all that magic makes

me tired."

Rosa's big, furry body slowly sat up, Rachel hanging around her neck like a massive necklace. Serafina had stepped back in amazement, staring as Rachel cuddled this huge, fierce-looking bear.

"Serafina, this is Rosa. Serafina is sleeping here tonight. She's going to help us." said Ian.

Rosa looked at Serafina, whose normal confidence had drained away.

"Thank you for helping, Serafina. It is very nice of you. Ian and Rachel have told me lots about you." Rosa touched Serafina's arm with her paw.

Ian took the plastic bag from Serafina's limp arms. He showed Rosa the hellebore herb that Serafina had been looking after. Rosa looked into the bag, taking it from Ian with her big paws.

"Ninos. Que sorpresa! What a surprise! How can I ever thank you? You are so wonderfully kind to me."

"Rosa," Rachel let go of Rosa's neck, "what are you going to do with the herb?"

Rosa laughed. "Why I am going to eat it, mi nina."

"Eat it!" Rachel was horrified. "But it's poisonous. The lady at the church said so. You might die."

Rosa's voice became serious. "I will not die. I have the magic to make me be alive still," Then seeing the excited look on Rachel's face she added. "You must all promise never to eat any of it. Without the magic it would make you very ill and Rachel is right, it could even kill you."

They all solemnly promised never to eat it.

"Good. It is wonderful to see you all. It was so cold

and dark down there. It felt as if the whole world had forgotten me. You have all come to help me."

Rosa's eyes seemed to shine in the dark. Was she crying? She held out her arms from around Rachel, who had snuggled back into her fur, pulling Ian and an astonished Serafina into her body, to hug them too.

Then, as if remembering where they were and what they had to do, she put the children down, gently disentangling Rachel from around her neck.

"Come now, we have work. We must go outside. The magic needs the power of the starlight."

Ian looked at Serafina and Rachel.

"We'll have to get our coats." It would be absolutely freezing outside. He led the way along the corridor to the coat rack under the stairs.

"Shoes as well," said Ian.

"I don't like shoes without socks," complained Rachel. "It makes my feet feel funny."

"Listen Rachel, it's freezing outside. Your slippers are no good. They're old and worn out. You have to wear your shoes," ordered Ian.

Rachel looked sharply at Ian. Serafina intervened. She had recovered from the shock of meeting Rosa.

"It's not for long, Rachel. We're not going to walk far, are we, Rosa?"

"We need a very big open space. Where can we go?" Rosa asked.

"How about the garden? Will that do?"

"Yes, Ian. We need to go pronto, now."

Ian led the way once more, heading further down

the corridor to the back door of the restaurant, where they always went in and out. They stood quietly waiting, holding their plastic bags, as he pulled back the big bolts. He took the key from his zipped up inside pocket, where he always kept it, and quietly undid the lock. He pushed the door open. It moved, without a sound, on well-oiled hinges.

They walked out into an icy world of white. Breathing in was like inhaling a cold fire of frozen flames. It hurt their lungs, until they got used to it. Their breath was clouded smoke, like old-fashioned steam trains.

It was very still. There was no movement at this hour, in the middle of such a cold, frosty night. The faint noise their footsteps made seemed incredibly loud as they crunched on the frosted, white concrete of the yard. Nothing else moved in the still night.

The garden gleamed palely in the starlight. The bright streetlamps at the front of the restaurant did not reach this far.

The park beyond the garden was a place of contrasts: the dark of purple tree shadows and the white of frosted grass that reached up the hill before joining onto the black, velvet sky.

There were no lights from the park and the restaurant fences screened them from the other buildings on either side of the garden.

They walked out from the yard, crushing the white grass and leaving dark footprints behind them. They didn't talk; the cold had stolen their breath away.

Rosa stopped. She took the bags, one by one, from

the children's icy hands, setting out their contents on the pale grass. With fumbling claws she put the stones and earth in each glass, before placing them in the shape of a square about three metres away from each other. Taking the fat candles from Ian's bag, she pushed each one gently into the soft earth inside the glasses. She took some of the rosemary that Ian had found in the kitchen, and carefully placed some on each candle.

"Ian, light the candles," ordered Rosa. The lovely, clean smell of rosemary cut into the air. Using her claws Rosa drew some strange signs on the white-coated grass outside the square.

The children watched, fascinated, as she did this: hypnotised by her slow deliberate movements. She walked around the square, murmuring things in a language that was not English or Spanish.

She stopped suddenly and stepped into the square, as if a door had opened.

Taking the hellebore herb she had carried with her, Rosa carefully picked several of its leaves. After rubbing them onto her face and paws she slipped them into her mouth and chewed them slowly before swallowing.

Going over to the side of the square nearest to them, she spoke to the children as though she were somewhere far away, her voice echoing softly from far off walls.

"The crystal, Ian. I need the crystal."

Ian turned to Rachel, holding out his freezing hand. Rachel soundlessly put her hand inside her coat and pulled out the crystal from her pyjama pocket. She hesitated a moment. Was she about to say something? Somehow the words wouldn't come out of her throat. She looked strangely at Ian. Her lips moved, but no sound came from them. She looked at Rosa, who smiled her fierce bear smile. Rachel smiled back a strangely sad smile and, with a sigh, put the crystal into Ian's waiting hand.

Ian walked towards Rosa and then unexpectedly stopped. He seemed to think for a moment. It was then that he did something that Rachel would remember for the rest of her life. Walking back, he took Rachel's hand and put the crystal into it. He pushed her towards the square, in the direction of Rosa's outstretched paw.

Rachel looked at him in amazement. She couldn't believe Ian was doing this for her. She went to the square holding out the crystal to Rosa. Rosa didn't take the crystal; instead she held open an invisible door.

Rachel walked into the square with the crystal and stood by Rosa. Their bodies became slightly blurred, as if they were in the distance, although they stayed the same size.

Rosa stood Rachel in the centre of the square and Rachel held the crystal out at arms' length. Then something extraordinary happened.

The crystal in Rachel's hand began to shine and four beams of light flashed out from it towards the candles in their glasses.

Gradually, in slow motion, the candle flames were drawn along the beams of light, changing into long strands of pure white. The beams reached the crystal at the same time. Immediately rainbows flowed out from the crystal.

Swiftly, like multicoloured rivers of water, the rainbows joined to each candle. The separate candles then drew out rainbows from each other, joining to make a square of moving, rainbow light.

Rachel held the shining crystal high above her head. She became the centre of the twisting, changing, rainbow square, covered in sparkling rainbow light. The diagonal rainbow rivers joined her to the corners of the dazzling square.

Rosa had stood perfectly still while this took place. Now she moved into the rainbow light. As soon as the rainbows touched her, she became a rainbow herself, the colours sinking into her fur, passing through her body again and again, until she was a rainbow, the colours flowing through her, wrapping around her, as she walked around Rachel through one rainbow stream after another. Both of them bathed in rainbows.

Gradually, Rachel floated up from the ground, turning the flat square into a pyramid of multicoloured light.

Rachel was laughing soundlessly, and she glowed from head to toe in an ever-changing waterfall of rainbow colour that flowed down over her head from the crystal.

Rosa stood beneath Rachel, under this cascade of colour. She twisted and turned her body in the rainbow waterfall that fell from Rachel. She washed and bathed in the light, rubbing it all over her as if under the shower. Serafina and Ian watched, transfixed, unable to move.

Then slowly they grew aware of a sound. It too seemed

to come from far away. Quietly at first, it built up into a song of amazing beauty. They had heard nothing like it in the entire world.

It reached inside them with its almost unbearable beauty, making them all want to laugh for joy and cry with sadness at the same time. Passing through and through them, it grew louder and louder, their bodies vibrated and tingled as the sound rose and fell like something alive inside them.

This was so strange and unknown to them that fear might easily have crept into their minds. But they knew, as the living sound whirled and surged within them, that this was something so good, so right and positive that it could never harm or hurt anyone or anything. This force existed only to be good and to do good to all who came into contact with it.

Then as they watched, Rosa slowly began to change before their disbelieving eyes.

As the rainbow splashed over her, the bulky bear's shape was washed away and her body stretched out into a big, bulky human shape. Despite the changing colours that drenched her body, they could now recognise the outline of a large woman.

Dark fur dissolved into rainbow-coloured clothes: beautiful, embroidered clothes. Long, tightly curled hair cascaded over her shoulders.

Rosa was a woman once more.

The rainbows still flowed around the pyramid, but now their speed slackened. Slowly the beautiful sound dropped to a murmur and stopped.

Rachel gradually sank to the ground. The pyramid turned back into a square. The rainbow colours gave way to white light. The crystal glow faded.

The candle flames returned to normal, dropping back into the glasses at each corner of the square.

As they did so, there was a strange cry from Rosa. She fell on the ground, turning and twisting in a blur of movement. She rolled out of the square into the shadows and lay still.

Rachel slumped to the floor, still clutching the crystal. The magic was gone. Released from its spell, Ian lurched forward and ran jerkily on frozen legs to Rachel, followed by Serafina who staggered over to Rosa.

Rachel sat up. "What happened? Where's Rosa?"

Ian looked across to where Rosa was being helped up by Serafina. Something was wrong though. The big, beautiful lady was gone and Rosa was a bear again! A groan escaped from his lips.

It hadn't worked. What had gone wrong.

A loud crash pulled them back to reality. The back door of the restaurant, which they had forgotten to close, had slammed.

Their attention had been fixed so closely on the rainbow pyramid that they hadn't noticed a freezing breeze growing in the cold night air. The slam of the door had shattered the silence.

Would it wake the sleeping restaurant? A sudden light shone from a bedroom window.

"Oh no," said Ian, "Mum and Dad have woken up." Swiftly he dragged Rachel towards the bushes, by the trees. The shadows there would hide them. They crouched silently, huddled behind the undergrowth. The sound of the window opening was followed by the click of a torch. Its white beam crossed the trampled, frosty lawn. It flashed over their hiding place. They heard the click as it was switched off and the muttering voice of Ian's dad.

"Nothing there," He paused. "I've no idea. An animal, perhaps." The voice was cut off as the window closed.

"We must get back in quickly. Before they discover we're not in bed. Come on, Rosa," said Ian. Rosa did not move. She looked at Ian

"I cannot, Ian. I must return to mi casa, I must go home."

"But you're still a bear!" Rachel's voice wailed into the night.

She sounded helplessly disappointed, about to cry. This could not be happening. They had tried so hard to get everything exactly right. Rosa had changed in the rainbow light. They had seen her transformation into a woman. What had gone wrong? Rosa hugged them as she always did.

"I think I understand what is happening ninos. This is noche, the night. I am always a bear at night. The magic has worked. I am sure it has, but I have been a bear for a long time. I think I must now wait until the dawn of the new day. I will turn back then. I am sure of this. I cannot go in with you. I must find my way home."

The children stared at her in sadness, sorrow written on their faces. Rosa could feel their distress.

100

"It is the time for saying adios, goodbye. You have been so good to me. I love you, all three of you. Without your helping I could not never turn back,"

Rosa was getting her words muddled up.

"We must all go back to our own worlds. I need to go home to Espana. You understand?"

She hugged them tightly.

"I must go and follow my path."

They held onto her, not wanting her to leave. She carefully shook herself free and touched each of them on the cheek with her warm tongue. They stood there until she pushed them gently towards the house.

They walked slowly, deliberately, not wanting to go, knowing they must. They stumbled towards the back door. They were happy for Rosa, but sad for her leaving. It took them some time to reach the restaurant.

Turning, they looked back to see Rosa waving at them from the shadows. They waved back. Ian pulled open the door and they walked in.

The silence in the restaurant was deafening.

It shrieked at them. "Rosa is gone. Rosa is gone." Tired and alone, they went to bed. The closing of their bedroom doors sealing them each into their own thoughts.

Just as he was about to get into bed, Ian took a last look out of the window. He could see across the frosty lawn, with its dark shadows where they had crushed the grass. As he watched, Rosa walked out from the shadows of the trees. She crossed the lawn, clambered over the garden fence and disappeared into the park beyond.

He watched for a while, hoping to see her once more.

As he stood there, he thought. What if Rosa didn't turn back? What if it had all gone completely wrong? Even if she did change, how would she get back to Spain? Spain was a long way away.

As he stared and wondered, there was Rosa again, standing near the top of the hill, her dark shape silhouetted against the white frost. Then before he could do anything, she was gone.

Rosa was gone.

Would he ever see her again? They had done their best to help her and she had loved them for it. It seemed silly, but something inside him knew that they would all meet again. How and when he did not know. He just knew they would meet once more.

With that thought in his mind he climbed into bed. Snuggling down under the covers he soon fell asleep.

He dreamed of walking through a forest with Rachel and Serafina, under a hot sun, a bear walking beside them, a big brown bear, which smiled a big bear's smile at him. As they walked, the bear laughed its fierce, rumbling laugh.

Suddenly they heard a familiar watery sound and instantly, walking beside them was a big, beautiful lady, with long black tightly curled hair that fell about her shoulders. Her wonderfully embroidered dress swirled in the breeze as she slowly turned and smiled a beautiful smile at them.

THE END

Look out for;

The Restaurant Bear Returns

By Colin Taylor

The exciting conclusion to the
Restaurant Bear story…

www.ingramcontent.com/pod-product-compliance
Lightning Source LLC
Chambersburg PA
CBHW050805250626
47155CB00005B/2214